BUILD HIGHER

BUILD HIGHER

Story by

AJ Reisman

Illustrated by

Soukina Abou Khalil

gatekeeper press™
Columbus, Ohio

Build Higher

Published by Gatekeeper Press
2167 Stringtown Rd, Suite 109
Columbus, OH 43123-2989
www.GatekeeperPress.com

The cover design and typesetting for this book are entirely the product of the author. Gatekeeper Press did not participate in and is not responsible for any aspect of these elements.

Library of Congress Control Number: 2020949353

ISBN (hardcover): 9781662906299
ISBN (paperback): 9781662906305

Thank you to my daughters for inspiring me to see the world as a child again.

Thank you mom for never charging me for proofreading.

Thank you to my wife Cara, lifelong friend Corey, and my devoted readers for your everlasting encouragement.

Thank you Seth Godin for inspiring me to write.

-AJ Reisman

Thank you to my family. I dedicate this to anyone who has ever felt they weren't already enough.

-Soukina Abou Khalil

Elie and Joey are building a tower

of blocks with their cat Squeaky.

Squeaky says, "Build higher."

So Elie and Joey build higher.

Squeaky says, "Build even higher!"

Elie and Joey build higher than
any other building around.

They build the Empire State Building!

"Build higher!" Squeaky shouts.
"Higher than the Empire
State Building.
Keep going until you reach the clouds."

So Elie and Joey build

higher

and

higher

and somehow they do

reach the clouds.

When they reach the
clouds, Squeaky says,
"Build higher. Build higher
than the clouds."

"Build until you reach the moon,"

Squeaky tells them.

They build...

And they build...

And somehow they do reach the moon.

When they reach the moon, Squeaky yells, "Build higher!"

Joey asks, "How can we build higher than the moon? The sky goes on and on forever."

"Should we build to Saturn, the Sun, or to the farthest star in the sky?", Elie asks.

Elie and Joey begin to build
higher and higher.

Squeaky climbs to the very
top and suddenly screams,

"I'm too high. I'm scared.

Get me down! Meow!"

Elie and Joey help him down.
Then Squeaky knocks down
the tower of blocks.

Elie and Joey begin to
rebuild their tower.

This time, they build it their own way,
not the way Squeaky tells them to.

Only then do Elie and Joey
realize that their tower of blocks
was already high enough.

CPSIA information can be obtained
at www.ICGtesting.com
Printed in the USA
LVHW070422011121
702040LV00002B/52